Zoe's Rescue Zoo

At first, all Zoe could see was a small, fluffy white bundle. Then the bundle moved, and a little white face with big dark eyes and furry ears was staring back at her. "It's a baby polar bear!" cried Zoe.

Look out for:

Zoe's Rescue ZOO

The Pesky Polar Bear

Amelia Cobb

Illustrated by **Sophy Williams**

nosy crow

First published in the UK in 2015 by Nosy Crow Ltd
The Crow's Nest, 10a Lant St
London, SE1 1QR, UK

Nosy Crow and associated logos are trademarks and/or
registered trademarks of Nosy Crow Ltd

Text copyright © Hothouse Fiction, 2015
Illustrations © Sophy Williams, 2015

The right of Hothouse Fiction and Sophy Williams to be identified as the author
and illustrator respectively of this work has been asserted by them in accordance
with the Copyright, Designs and Patents Act 1988.

A CIP catalogue record for this book will be available from the British Library

Printed and bound in the UK by Clays Ltd, St Ives Plc

Papers used by Nosy Crow are made from wood grown in sustainable forests.

ISBN: 978 0 85763 440 5

www.nosycrow.com

Chapter One

Panda Playtime

Zoe Parker shivered and pulled her coat around her. "Brrr! It's really chilly today!" she said.

"Chi Chi and Mei Mei don't seem to mind!" replied Stephanie, the panda keeper. "Their thick furry coats must be keeping them nice and warm."

It was a wintry Sunday morning at

the Rescue Zoo, and Zoe was helping
Stephanie in the panda enclosure. They
each had a watering can and were
sprinkling water over the bamboo plants.
The Rescue Zoo pandas, Chi Chi and
Mei Mei, liked lots of different fruits, nuts
and seeds, but the juicy, green bamboo
growing in their enclosure was their
favourite thing to eat. And, like all pandas,
they munched lots of it!

"They're really playful this morning,
aren't they?" said Zoe, as Chi Chi chased
her little sister across the enclosure,
squeaking excitedly as she dashed right
under Stephanie's feet! Stephanie cried
out in surprise, wobbled and almost lost
her balance, grabbing on to a tree to keep
herself from falling over.

"That was close!" she laughed. "I've

almost tripped over them once already
this morning, the cheeky little things."

Zoe loved helping Stephanie look after the pandas. Whenever she had any spare time at all she could be found in the zoo: helping out the zookeepers or playing with the animals! But Zoe wasn't a visitor, like most people who passed through the zoo gates – she actually *lived* at the Rescue Zoo! Her Great-Uncle Horace was a famous explorer and animal expert, and he had built the zoo so that all the lost, frightened and injured animals he met on his travels would have somewhere safe to live.

Zoe's mum, Lucy, was the zoo vet. Lucy and Zoe lived in a little cottage at the edge of the zoo, so that whenever an animal was poorly or injured, Lucy was close by and could quickly help them. Zoe thought she was the luckiest girl

in the world to have so many amazing
animals right outside her front door!

"Yum. I wasn't sure I'd like bamboo,
but it's very tasty!" chirped a little
voice behind her. Zoe turned to see a
little, furry creature with
big golden eyes nibbling
happily at a green shoot.
Glancing over to check
that Stephanie wasn't
close enough to hear, she
whispered with a smile,
"Naughty Meep. If Chi
Chi and Mei Mei spot
you eating their
bamboo, they'll be
very cross!"

Living at the
Rescue Zoo

wasn't the only special thing about Zoe. On her sixth birthday, she had found out that animals can understand people. And Zoe had discovered that *she* had a special ability to understand animals, and talk back! No one else knew the secret, though – it was between her and the animals.

Zoe had lots of animal friends, but Meep was her *best* friend. He was a small, soft and very cheeky grey mouse lemur. He had come to the zoo when he was just a baby. He was too tiny to be on his own, and so had stayed in the cottage with Zoe and her mum ever since!

Meep finished his bamboo and scampered up on to Zoe's shoulder. "The pandas didn't see! They're too busy playing," he chattered.

Zoe laughed as the little pandas rolled along the ground, squealing excitedly. They were so cute! When the sisters had first arrived at the Rescue Zoo, they hadn't got along very well, but now they were great friends and always had fun together.

"That gives me an idea," Zoe whispered to Meep. "Maybe we could ask the pandas if they have any ideas about how we can celebrate Mum's birthday!"

It was Lucy's birthday in a few days time. Zoe thought that must be why her mum always seemed so happy at this time of year. Most people didn't like wet, cold, shivery January – but Lucy loved getting wrapped up in warm layers, going for snowy walks and cuddling down with a mug of hot chocolate in the evening.

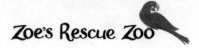

Stephanie called to Zoe from the other side of the enclosure. "Zoe, I need to fetch some special plant food for the bamboo. I won't be long."

Perfect, thought Zoe. *Now I can talk to the twins without Stephanie being around.*
Zoe had to be careful not to let her secret slip! "OK," she replied, waving. "Bye!"

As soon as Stephanie was out of sight,

Zoe turned to the pandas. "Chi Chi and Mei Mei! Listen – it's my mum's birthday soon, and I don't know how to help her celebrate. Do you have any ideas?"

Chi Chi squeaked excitedly and grabbed a handful of bamboo, while Mei Mei scampered eagerly to a bush and hid behind it, before peeping out, squeaking her own answer to Zoe.

Zoe burst out laughing. "A birthday feast of bamboo, and then a game of hide-and-seek?" she said, giving them both a cuddle. "You two are so funny. Those are lovely ideas, but I think they might be better for little pandas than grown-up people!"

"If Goo was here, we could ask him," chirped Meep. Goo was the little lemur's nickname for Great-Uncle Horace, which he found hard to say.

Zoe nodded. "That's true, Meep. He always has good ideas for birthdays." She touched the silver necklace she wore around her neck, which had a little paw-print charm hanging from it. It had been a birthday present from Great-Uncle Horace and was very precious to her – particularly because the special charm opened every enclosure at the zoo!

Mei Mei nudged Zoe with her nose and squeaked hopefully.

Zoe smiled. "No, Mei Mei – I don't know where Great-Uncle Horace is right now," she explained, tickling the little panda gently under the chin. "I wish I did! I got a postcard from him two weeks ago. He was in Brazil, helping a toucan with a poorly beak, but he probably travelled somewhere else after that."

"I miss Goo. I hope he comes home soon," said Meep a little sadly, and both pandas squeaked in agreement.

"I miss Great-Uncle Horace too, but don't worry," Zoe told them. "I'm sure he wouldn't want to miss Mum's birthday!"

Chapter Two
A Speedy Arrival

Suddenly Meep's furry ears pricked up, and his eyes opened wide. "Zoe! What's that noise?"

Zoe listened. "I can't hear anything, Meep," she said. "Your amazing ears always hear things much sooner than mine!"

"It's a rumbling sound," Meep

explained. "A little bit like when the rhinos are snoring. But it's getting louder!"

The other animals nearby were starting to notice the noise too. Zoe could hear curious barks from the arctic wolves, snorts from the walruses and brays from the donkeys. Then there was a rustling sound as all the parakeets fluttered to the tops of the trees and perched on the highest branches to get a better look. They peered down, their beady eyes bright. Then they started to screech and squawk excitedly.

"Something's definitely going on, Meep!" said Zoe. "Let's go and have a look."

The little pandas bounced up and down, squeaking excitedly, wanting to know what was happening. "I promise we'll come back later and tell you everything," Zoe told them, patting Chi Chi and Mei Mei on their adorable heads. Then she and Meep dashed out of the enclosure and down the path, towards the noisy rumbling sound. "It's coming from the zoo gates!" Meep squeaked excitedly.

They raced around the last corner of the path, past the giraffes on one side and the kangaroos on the other. The tall wooden gates, covered in carvings of different animals, were wide open, and a shiny, cherry-red car was rolling through them. It was low to the ground with an open top, and cheery music was playing on the radio – and it was pulling a large wooden trailer behind it.

"So *that's* what was making the rumbling noise!" gasped Zoe. "Wow, Meep – that's the coolest car I've ever seen!"

Sitting in the front of the car was a man with untidy white hair, merry brown eyes and a beaming smile. Perched on the back of the seat next to him was a beautiful bird with deep-blue feathers and a long, curved beak.

"It's Great-Uncle Horace! And Kiki!"
exclaimed Zoe.

"Yay!" squeaked Meep, bouncing
around excitedly on the path. Zoe giggled
as her little friend turned three cartwheels
in a row. "Goo is back! Zoe, you said
he'd be home soon – and you were right!"

"And it looks like he's brought a new
animal back with him," Zoe added,
nodding at the wooden trailer. Her heart

started to beat fast with excitement. Most
of the time, Great-Uncle Horace returned
to the zoo when he had an animal who
needed a new home. The last time he
came back, he'd brought a family of
beautiful snow leopards – before that,
a gorgeous, silky seal pup and a cheeky
baby elephant. Zoe knew the zoo's newest
animal must be inside the trailer! But
what could it be?

"Hello, Zoe and Meep!" cried Great-
Uncle Horace, switching off the ignition
and climbing out of the car. Zoe rushed
over for a hug, and her great-uncle picked
her up and swung her round. "Goodness,
Zoe, I think you've grown even taller
since Christmas!"

"Uncle Horace!" called a happy voice
behind them. Zoe turned to see her mum

running over, her dark curly hair escaping
from its ponytail. A crowd of excited
zookeepers followed. "We heard the
commotion and guessed you might
be here. I'm so glad to see you. We've
missed you!"

Great-Uncle Horace hugged Lucy. "I've missed you all, too! It's so good to be home. We've travelled a long way."

"Where did you go this time?" Zoe asked eagerly.

"Well, after we helped our toucan friend in Brazil, we travelled to America! What an exciting place it is, Zoe – one day I'll take you there. First we went to New York, where I saw the famous Statue of Liberty. Then to San Diego, where I tried surfing! Well, some paddling anyway. And then we went to Hollywood, where all the film stars live."

"Is that where you got your new car?" asked Lucy with a smile.

Great-Uncle Horace nodded enthusiastically. "Do you like it? It has all sorts of clever gadgets. And a *very* useful

compartment where I keep my custard
creams," he added, showing Zoe how
it popped open and then taking out a
biscuit for each of them.

Meep started nibbling at his biscuit
right away, but Zoe had other things
on her mind. "Great-Uncle Horace,"
she asked hopefully, "what's inside that
wooden trailer?"

Great-Uncle Horace winked at her.
"I can see you're eager to meet our new
arrival, my dear!" he said. "She's come
all the way from a zoo in California!
They didn't have enough room for her –
although she's small now, she'll grow to
be very big one day. So they asked me if
I might be able to help. Of course, I said
yes straightaway."

Zoe's mind was racing as she tried

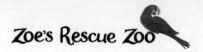

to guess what the animal was. A baby hippo? They were very small, but grew to be huge! Or a rhino maybe?

"There's a little window in the side of the trailer, Zoe," said Great-Uncle Horace, pointing. "Why don't you go and peep inside?"

Zoe felt nervous and excited all at the same time. What could be inside the trailer. . .?

Chapter Three
A Friend for Bella

At first, all Zoe could see was a small, fluffy white bundle. Then the bundle moved, and she saw a little white face with big dark eyes, furry ears and a black snout that was twitching with curiosity. "It's a baby polar bear!" cried Zoe.

"That's right! She's just eight weeks old,"

 23

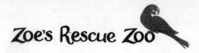
explained Great-Uncle Horace. "I knew
the Rescue Zoo would be the perfect
home for her, because we already have
the most beautiful polar bear enclosure,
with plenty of space for a new cub. And
inside the igloo, we've just refurbished the
swimming-pool area with a brand-new
viewing platform, of course – and added
the wonderful new play area!"

"Now Bella will have another polar
bear to play with!" said Zoe happily.
Bella was a gorgeous polar bear who had
come to the zoo a year ago, and she was
one of Zoe's special friends.

Great-Uncle Horace nodded. "I think
we should go and introduce them right
away! Zoe, why don't you hop in?"

"I'll find Jonny and tell him the news.
He'll be so excited!" said Lucy, grabbing

her walkie-talkie. Jonny was the polar-bear keeper who looked after Bella.

Zoe climbed into the shiny red car and fastened her seat belt. Meep perched on Zoe's shoulder, and Kiki flew overhead. As the car rumbled slowly through the zoo, Great-Uncle Horace beeped the horn and waved happily at all the visitors they passed. Everyone smiled and waved back.

The polar-bear enclosure was a wide, flat, snowy landscape dotted with tall fir trees, with a huge white igloo in the middle. There was the new play area outside the igloo, with lots of wooden platforms and ramps, tyres and brightly coloured rubber toys. Inside the igloo was a deep blue pool, and the new raised viewing platform ran all around

it, where visitors could watch Bella
splashing, swimming and diving. A snow
machine blew soft white snowflakes over
the whole enclosure, and kept it at the
perfect temperature all year round. As the
car pulled up outside it, Zoe saw Jonny
rushing over to the fence. He was always
wrapped up in a warm jumper and

bobble hat, even when it was the middle of summer, because he spent all day surrounded by ice and snow. "Mr Higgins! Welcome back!" he said, grinning. "It's such good news that Bella's going to have a friend! She's definitely ready to live with another, younger bear."

"Well, this little cub is very sweet,

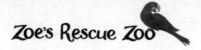

so hopefully they'll get along right away," said Great-Uncle Horace, hopping out of the car and holding open the door for Zoe and Meep. "Let's open the trailer so she can have a look at her new home."

Jonny and Great-Uncle Horace unfastened the bolts on the trailer door, and it swung open. Without a moment's hesitation, the little cub tumbled out. She looked around excitedly, her dark eyes bright, her little snout sniffing curiously and her fluffy tail wiggling. But then she scampered away out of the gate and down the path, away from the enclosure!

"Oh dear, she's off!" laughed Jonny, dashing after her.

"She's a bit of a handful, Zoe!" chuckled Great-Uncle Horace, turning to her and shaking his head.

Jonny managed to catch up with
the little bear, who was dashing from
enclosure to enclosure along the path in
the zoo, peering eagerly through each
fence to look at the other animals. Jonny
tried to guide her back towards her own
enclosure, but the bear was too excited
to pay any attention. She raced from the

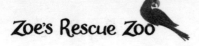

gazelles to the llamas and the peacocks, squealing happily at every new sight. Eventually Jonny bent down to try and scoop her up and carry her – but the cub scampered right through his legs, and dashed off in the other direction!

"Quick, Meep!" whispered Zoe, and they both hurried after her. Meep was tiny but very fast, and he reached the excited little bear first. "Wait!" he chattered. "You're going the wrong way!"

"Your new home is back there!" added Zoe as she reached Meep and the cub, panting. She glanced behind her to make sure Jonny wasn't close enough to hear. "Trust me – you'll love it."

"It's full of brilliant toys to play with," said Meep.

"And a great big pool to splash around

in. But best of all, there's another polar
bear, just like you. Her name is Bella!"
explained Zoe.

The bear suddenly stopped and stared
at Zoe, her big eyes very wide. Then she
gave a squeal of excitement, turned and
dashed back towards her enclosure. Jonny

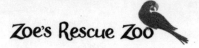

cheered as she raced through the open gate and into her new home. "You must have said the magic words!" he joked, smiling at Zoe.

Zoe grinned. She just hoped the little polar bear would be happy at the Rescue Zoo!

Chapter Four
A Snowy Surprise

"I've finished!" said Zoe, jumping up from the table and carrying her plate into the kitchen. "Can I go and visit the new polar bear now?"

Her mum laughed. "I don't think I've ever seen you eat your dinner so quickly, Zoe! Of course you can, but don't stay out too late – remember you've got

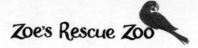

school tomorrow. I'll make you a hot
chocolate before bed."

Zoe flung on her coat, hat and scarf,
and gave her mum a kiss before she
rushed outside with Meep. In the evening
the zoo was lit by tall, curving lamps that
shone a gentle golden light on to the
paths. All the visitors had left by now, but
most of the zookeepers were still around,
finishing off their jobs before they went
home too. Lots of Zoe's animal friends

were still awake, and chirped, squawked
or trumpeted when they saw her
go past. It wasn't just the nocturnal
animals, who slept during the day and
woke up at night. Tonight *every* enclosure
seemed to be
buzzing with
chatter about
the new
arrival!

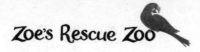

"It's a polar bear cub!" Zoe told Bertie, the excited little elephant, who was desperate to know what the new arrival was. "I'm going to visit her now!"

When Zoe arrived at the polar-bear enclosure, she was relieved to see that Jonny had already gone home for the evening. That meant she could chat to the polar bears without worrying that he might overhear her! She pulled out her special necklace from underneath her scarf, and held the paw-print charm against a little panel in the fence. There was a quiet click and the gate swung open for her.

As Zoe stepped inside, she felt the icy air blow gently against her cheeks, and her nose and ears tingled with the cold. "I'm glad I wrapped up warm, Meep!" she said.

Meep's teeth were chattering, so Zoe picked her little friend up and popped him in her coat pocket. Meep snuggled down happily, and peeped his head out so he could still see what was going on. "It's toasty in here!" he chirped.

Zoe looked around at the snowy ground and giggled. "Meep, look!" she said. Usually the snow lay in a perfectly smooth layer, like white icing on a cake, with just a few tracks to show where Bella had padded through it. But today the snow was scattered messily everywhere, covered in paw prints and squashed flat where the little bear had been rolling around.

"At least she seems to like it," chuckled Meep.

"I wonder what Bella thinks. She's such

37

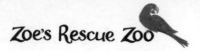

a neat and tidy little thing," said Zoe. "Oh look, Meep – there's the new cub!"

The smaller polar bear was playing with an inflatable ball over by the igloo. When she spotted Zoe and Meep, she bounded over to them, squealing and barking eagerly.

"Hello!" said Zoe, giggling as the cub leaped into her arms for a cuddle. Sometimes new animals were nervous or shy when they first arrived at the zoo, but not this one! "I'm Zoe. And this is my best friend, Meep. What's your name?"

The cub gave a proud little growl, her dark-brown eyes bright and excited.

"Snowy! That's the perfect name for you!" said Zoe, smiling. "Do you like your new home? I hope you're settling in – you had a long journey to get here!"

Snowy nodded eagerly, yapping and barking at the top of her voice. Zoe listened as the cub told her all about the zoo she had come from in America, the cosy trailer she had travelled to the Rescue Zoo in, and the brilliant pool she had splashed around in all afternoon. Her eyes lit up when she mentioned her special new friend, Bella.

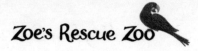

Just then, Zoe spotted the other polar bear padding over to join them. Bella was growing fast, although Zoe knew she wouldn't be fully grown until she was five or six. "Hi, Bella!" she called. "Snowy says you've been showing her around."

Bella nodded, and opened her mouth to reply. But Snowy started talking again before Bella could say anything, chattering away about Jonny, the kind man who had come to give her a lovely dinner.

The older bear looked surprised, and Zoe smiled at her. Bella was a kind and friendly bear, but she had always had the big enclosure to herself, and seemed a bit overwhelmed by noisy, excited Snowy.

"I know it must be strange, sharing your home with someone new," Zoe whispered quietly to Bella. "But I'm sure you and Snowy are going to get on really well."

Once Snowy had shown Zoe and Meep

41

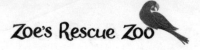

the cosy snow den that she would
sleep in, Zoe said goodbye to the polar
bears. "We've got to go home now, but
we'll come and see you tomorrow," she
promised, giving them both a cuddle.
As they left, making sure the gate was
properly shut behind them, Zoe could
still hear Snowy's excited squeals, and
laughed. "Snowy is so cute! But she's a
real chatterbox, isn't she?"

Meep nodded. "She's very excited!" he
chirped.

"She'll calm down once she's had
a good night's sleep. It's been a long
day," said Zoe. Suddenly she thought
of something. "Meep! With all the
excitement, we've still not thought of how
to celebrate Mum's birthday!"

"Mei Mei and Chi Chi had some good

ideas," remembered Meep. "Maybe we could ask all the other animals?"

"Good thinking, Meep!" Zoe rushed up to the nearest enclosure and peeped through the fence. The Rescue Zoo dolphins were enjoying an evening swim in the lake, and the smallest dolphin was playing happily with a red bouncy ball, flicking it high into the air with her nose.

"Hi, Coral," Zoe called. "Listen – it's my mum's birthday soon, and I don't know what to do. Do you have any ideas?"

Coral glided through the water towards Zoe, making a friendly clicking noise. "Give her a new ball and then play catch in the lake?" said Zoe, smiling. "That's a lovely idea – but I'm not sure it's right for my mum."

Suddenly there was a squawking noise

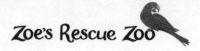
from the next enclosure. The Rescue Zoo macaws, Ruby and Cupid, had overheard and wanted to give Zoe *their* idea for a birthday present. Zoe peered through the fence and smiled at them. "That's a nice idea too," she told them, "but my mum already has a lovely bed to sleep in – so she doesn't need a wooden perch like yours. And you have clever, strong feet to grip it with. I think my mum would fall off!"

Zoe and Meep stopped at every enclosure they passed on the way home, and heard lots of ideas, but didn't think that any would be perfect for Zoe's mum. The zebras suggested some lovely hay to nibble, because that was their favourite treat, but Zoe knew her mum wouldn't like that very much. And she had

managed to hide her smile when Snappy
the crocodile suggested a new toothbrush
– he was very proud of his gleaming
white teeth! Meep was keen to ask all the
animals they hadn't talked to yet, but Zoe
shook her head. "We should go home,
Meep – it's getting late and Mum will
worry. I just wish we knew what to do! I
want it to be something really special –
something she'll love."

Meep wrinkled his tiny nose up as he
thought carefully. "What *does* she love?"

"Well, she loves the animals," said Zoe.
"She's always happiest when she's helping
Leonard the lion, or Alex the gorilla,
or the giraffes, or the dolphins. And just
like me, she loves it when Great-Uncle
Horace comes home from an adventure
and surprises us with a new animal for

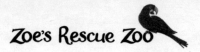

the zoo. . ." Zoe stopped suddenly. her eyes
bright. "Meep, that's it! She loves *surprises*.
I think we should throw her a surprise
birthday party!"

Chapter Five
Zoe's Party Plan

After school the next day, Zoe and Meep raced over to Higgins Hall. "Great-Uncle Horace? It's me!" called Zoe, pushing open the huge front door.

Whenever he was home from his travels, Great-Uncle Horace lived in the big house that had belonged to his family for a really long time. It sat on a hill overlooking the zoo, and looked very grand from the outside. And inside it was the strangest house Zoe had ever seen!

Great-Uncle Horace had turned almost every room into a home for animals. Some pelicans lived in the swimming pool, and tiny tropical frogs hopped around the bathroom. Zoe's favourite was the old ballroom, where elegant parties were held long ago. It was now where the Rescue Zoo butterflies lived – including a very rare pink and white butterfly that Great-Uncle Horace had discovered himself, and had named after Zoe!

"Zoe, my dear, how lovely!" Great-Uncle Horace called back cheerily. "I'm in the library."

Zoe walked inside, with Meep perched on her shoulder. Great-Uncle Horace was

sitting in a cosy old armchair, sipping
a cup of tea and nibbling a biscuit. All
around him, lush plants and bushes were
growing where books used to be, and tiny,
colourful hummingbirds were darting and
buzzing among them. "Take a seat! And

do have a custard cream!" Great-Uncle
Horace said, patting the chair next to him
and passing her a plate of biscuits. "Now,
what can I do for you, Zoe? You look
as though you have something on your
mind."

"Well, it's Mum's birthday soon," Zoe
began. "And I thought it might be really
fun to throw her a surprise party. She
loves surprises! What do you think?"

"I think that's a wonderful idea!" cried
Great-Uncle Horace. "I haven't been to
a surprise party in years. Goodness, how
exciting. Will there be birthday cake?" he
added hopefully.

Zoe giggled. "I thought I could ask the
zookeepers to bake one," she said.

Great-Uncle Horace nodded eagerly.
"And I can help you make the

invitations," he told her. "But where is the party going to be held?"

"I think we should have it somewhere in the zoo," Zoe explained. "But it's so busy in the daytime with all the visitors."

Great-Uncle Horace scratched his head, looking thoughtful. "Perhaps we could open the zoo a little later than usual that day?" he suggested. "But I'm afraid you'd have to ask Mr Pinch's permission."

Mr Pinch was the manager of the zoo, and the biggest spoilsport Zoe had ever met! He was always grumbling about the meerkats making a mess, or the chimps being cheeky. Zoe's heart sank. She loved Great-Uncle Horace's idea to open the zoo late, so they had lots of time to enjoy the party – but would Mr Pinch say yes?

Zoe and Meep finished their biscuits,

 51

said goodbye to Great-Uncle Horace and then went off to find the zoo manager.

"Promise to behave yourself, Meep," Zoe said. "We need Mr Pinch to be in the best mood possible."

The little lemur grudgingly agreed. Meep loved to be especially cheeky to the zoo manager, so they didn't get along very well!

Soon they arrived at Mr Pinch's office. It was right in the middle of the zoo, just past the hippos' muddy lagoon. Zoe took a deep breath, crossed her fingers for luck and knocked on the door.

"Who is it?" a grumpy voice answered. "I'm very busy, you know!"

Zoe pushed open the door. Mr Pinch was sitting at his desk with a pile of papers in front of him. His uniform was perfectly ironed, and his shoes and hat polished to a shine. He frowned when he saw Meep, right behind Zoe.

"Hello, Mr Pinch," said Zoe politely.

"It's just me. I wanted to talk to you about my mum's birthday. It's in a few days and I'd like to organise a surprise party for her. Great-Uncle Horace we wondered if we could open the zoo a little late that day, so that everyone can help with the party food and the decorations—"

"A party!" interrupted Mr Pinch, groaning. "A messy, noisy party! No doubt *I* will have to organise everything, and then clean up afterwards. No, definitely not. I already have enough to do. Did you know that those naughty monkeys threw banana skins all over the path this morning? An extremely dangerous thing to do – I slipped on one and very nearly landed right on my bottom, just as a big group of visitors walked past! I had to spend the next half an hour picking up all of the banana skins while the cheeky creatures blew rude raspberries at me from behind the fence!"

Meep gave a noisy snigger as Mr Pinch turned back to his paperwork. Zoe managed to hide her smile, and shook her head quickly at the little lemur. "If you make him cross, we'll never be able to change his mind about the party," she whispered. "Shhh, Meep!"

Zoe tried again to persuade the grumpy zoo manager. "That's very naughty of the monkeys, but I promise you won't have to tidy up anything once it's over – we'll make sure everything is spotless." She paused, then added, "I think my mum really deserves a party, Mr Pinch. She's always rushing around looking after the animals, and it would be so nice to do something lovely for her. Please can we open a little bit late, just this once?"

Zoe waited hopefully, and Meep wore his most innocent expression. Mr Pinch sighed. "Oh, very well. I suppose we can open late on this occasion. I can see you won't leave my office until I agree!"

Zoe breathed a sigh of relief. "Thanks, Mr Pinch! It will be fun, honestly!" she told him, skipping out of his office and pretending not to hear him grumbling behind her.

"Hooray!" cried Meep, bouncing up and down on Zoe's shoulder. "We're going to have a party!"

"Now we just need to decide *where* to have it," Zoe said. "It needs to be

somewhere big
enough for lots of
people."

"Somewhere
not too muddy,"
chirped Meep.
"So not
the hippos'
lagoon, or
the warthogs'
field."

"And not the pot-bellied pigs' enclosure
either. They're so greedy that they'd eat
all the party food before anyone arrived,"
added Zoe, giggling.

"What about the elephants' enclosure?"
suggested Meep. "It's big enough, and
Oscar and Bertie could use their trunks to
help us put up decorations!"

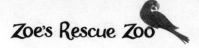

"That's true, Meep, but Mum walks past that enclosure every day on her way to the zoo hospital," pointed out Zoe. "So we couldn't make the party a surprise. She'd notice all the balloons and guess what was going on! No, we need somewhere she won't see what's happening inside while we set up the surprise..." Suddenly she snapped her fingers. "Meep, I've got it! The igloo in the polar-bear enclosure would be the perfect place! There's the special platform inside it – we could have the party there."

"Won't everyone be cold?" pointed out Meep, his teeth starting to chatter at the thought of it.

"We'll make sure we put *'wear lots of warm clothes!'* on the party invitations," said Zoe. "We could give the party a lovely winter theme, with snowy decorations and treats, because it's Mum's favourite time of year. Meep, I'm so excited now. This is going to be the best party *ever*!"

Chapter Six
Polar Bear Problems

Zoe and Meep raced straight to the polar bear enclosure. "I can't wait to tell Bella and Snowy about the party," said Zoe as she opened the gate with her special necklace. "They'll be so excited!"

When they arrived, Snowy was gliding around in the pool and Bella was eating some silvery fish for dinner. They both

barked eagerly when they saw Zoe and
Meep. "It's nice to see you too!" laughed
Zoe. "Listen, I've got something to tell
you. We're throwing a surprise birthday
party for my mum. And it's going to be
right here – in your igloo!"

Bella clapped her paws together
excitedly and Snowy splashed around,
yapping and squealing with glee. Both
bears were delighted that they were going
to be at the party themselves and would
see all the fun. "I thought the viewing
platform would be the perfect spot," Zoe
explained. "We'll have party food and
decorations up there. And I'll make sure
there are treats for both of you, too!"

Snowy barked noisily, still splashing her
paws in the water excitedly. "Party games
and a polar bear show! Those are lovely

ideas," said Zoe. "What about you, Bella?
Is there anything special you think we
should have at the party?"

Bella gave an eager bark, starting
to make some suggestions. But Snowy
interrupted her with an excited squeal,
splashed out of the pool and scampered
right up to Zoe to
make sure she had
her full attention.
"The polar bear
show sounds
brilliant, Snowy,"

Zoe reassured the excited little cub. "And if you used to perform it at your old zoo in America, I bet you're really good at it! But let's listen to Bella's ideas too, and then we can choose what to do."

But the pesky little bear wouldn't let Bella have her turn. She rushed over to the older bear, chattering eagerly about the show she wanted them to perform, and bouncing around excitedly. Zoe watched anxiously, and even Meep looked worried. "Bella looks really annoyed!" he whispered to Zoe.

"Snowy is only little. She doesn't understand that she needs to listen, too," Zoe whispered back. "Luckily, Bella is being really patient with her."

But just as Zoe spoke, it seemed that Bella's patience ran out! The cross polar

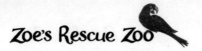

bear huffed loudly and then pushed the
little cub away with her paw. Giving a
moody growl, Bella slunk sulkily away
to her sleeping area.

"Oh dear!" Zoe and Meep rushed over
to Snowy, who was staring after Bella
in confusion. She gave a sad little squeal.
The cub didn't understand what she had
done wrong!

"Don't worry, Snowy," Meep said, cuddling up to her.

"Bella is just a bit tired," Zoe reassured her. But deep down, she thought Bella *was* cross with the little cub – and Zoe didn't know what to do about it. How could she make Snowy understand that she had to learn to listen? And would the squabbling polar bears be friends in time for the party?

Chapter Seven
Sad Snowy

"That's the invitations done!" said Zoe, holding up a neat stack of cards to show Great-Uncle Horace.

"Excellent, Zoe! Our glittery snowflake design looks fantastic!" Great-Uncle Horace said. "And you made those marvellous party hats yourself, too," he added, looking very impressed.

It was a day later, and Zoe was at Higgins Hall after school so she could make a start on the party decorations without her mum seeing. She had her pencil case and box of craft things open, and she spread out coloured paper, pens and pencils, fabric and glitter all over the table in the butterfly room. Meep was trying to help, but making lots of mess.

"Meep, there's glitter all over your face – and blue paint on your tail!" chuckled Zoe when Great-Uncle Horace had left the room. "We'll have to wash that off before we go home. If Mum sees it, she might get suspicious! Now, where has the sticky tape gone?"

Meep looked around and pointed at the floor. "Look, Zoe!"

Zoe glanced down. "Oh, Herbert, you

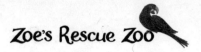

cheeky thing!"

A group of the tortoises that lived at the
Hall had come into the room when they
heard Zoe was there, keen to say hello.
They had started playing with a roll of
sticky tape, nudging it along with their
heads and waddling slowly after it. "I
promise I'll give it straight back, Herbert,"
Zoe told the smallest tortoise, who

squeaked indignantly when Zoe picked
the roll up. "I just need one last piece
to finish this bunting. There! What do
you think?" She held the line of bunting
up to show them. She had used three
different shades of blue paper to make the
triangles, and had drawn stars, snowflakes
and the letter "L" for Lucy on them
with a silver pen. The tortoises squeaked
approvingly, and Meep clapped his tiny
hands.

"Can we go and put it up now, Zoe?
Can we?" the little lemur asked.

"Not yet, Meep, but we can go and
hide all the decorations we've made in
the polar-bear enclosure," Zoe told him.
"There's a store cupboard next to the
swimming pool that will be perfect –
Mum would never look in there. And we

can see how Snowy and Bella are doing. Hopefully they'll have made up and become friends again today!"

Zoe put all the invitations and decorations carefully in her school bag, making sure nothing got squashed. She scooped the tortoises up and took them back to their home in the conservatory, then called goodbye to Great-Uncle Horace as she left the Hall.

"Will there be lots of tasty things to eat at the party, Zoe?" asked Meep hopefully as they made their way to the polar-bear enclosure. "Lots of yummy seeds and nuts and fruit?"

Zoe chuckled. "Oh, Meep, you're always hungry! Yes, the zookeepers are in charge of the party food. Will is making ice lollies, Frankie is baking cupcakes and gingerbread, and Jess is going to bake a big birthday cake with lots of scrummy white chocolate icing."

Meep squealed excitedly. "Yum! I wish it was the party right now, Zoe!"

When they got to the polar-bear enclosure, Zoe was about to reach for her paw-print necklace, but she stopped quickly at the fence. "Meep!" she hissed. "Look – Mum's here! It's a good job we hid all the other party decorations."

"What's she doing here?" whispered Meep. "Is one of the polar bears poorly?"

"I hope not," replied Zoe, suddenly feeling worried. "Let's go and see."

Inside the enclosure, Lucy was putting her stethoscope back in her special vet's bag. "Hello, love!" she called when she saw Zoe. "Jonny asked me to come and

have a look at Snowy because she's not
been eating very well."

Zoe looked at Snowy in surprise. The
cub was curled up in a little ball, sniffling.
Bella was nowhere to be seen, so Zoe
knew she must be swimming in the pool.
"Is there something wrong with Snowy?"
she asked her mum.

Lucy shook her head. "No, nothing at
all! She's perfectly healthy. It's strange."
She gave Snowy's fluffy head a stroke.
"Jonny will be keeping a close eye on her,
and if she doesn't start eating properly
I'll have to come back and check on her
again. It can be really dangerous for cubs
as small as Snowy not to eat enough."

When Lucy had packed up the rest of
her things and was ready to leave, Zoe
hesitated. She wanted to talk to the little

polar bear and find out what was going on. "Can I stay and play with the polar bears for a bit?" she asked.

"OK, but make sure you're home for tea in half an hour," Lucy told her.

When she had disappeared down the path, Zoe and Meep rushed over to Snowy. "What's wrong?" Zoe asked. "Mum says you haven't been eating properly."

"Don't you like the fish here?" asked Meep.

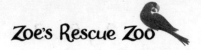

Snowy just sniffed sadly. Zoe moved
closer to the little polar bear. "Come on,
Snowy. Tell us what's going on," she said
gently.

Snowy glanced behind her towards the

pool and gave a small, miserable squeal.

"Oh, Snowy, that's not true! Of course Bella likes you," Zoe said. "Please don't say you wish you'd never left your old zoo in America. I hate to think of you being unhappy here!"

In a tiny voice, Snowy explained that Bella wouldn't listen to her ideas about the show that Snowy wanted them to perform at the party – and the bigger cub kept growling and being cross with her.

Zoe patted Snowy softly. She knew that animals sometimes lost their appetites when they were sad – just like people. "Listen, Snowy, I promise that things will get better. Bella just needs to get used to sharing her home with someone new. She's used to living alone, in peace and quiet. It must be strange and different for

 75

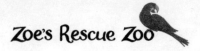

her too." Zoe paused. She didn't want to upset the little cub by telling her that she was annoying Bella! "It's lovely that you're excited about your new home, but sometimes you get a bit . . . *over* excited," she added gently.

But Snowy just let out another miserable squeak and slunk off towards her bed. Zoe sighed. "Meep, this is awful. If the polar bears don't make friends soon, Snowy won't eat properly and might become ill. And that would be terrible."

Meep had thought of something else too. "And if she gets poorly, your mum will have to come and check on her lots," he pointed out. "And that means. . ."

"The surprise party!" gasped Zoe. "We'll never be able to plan it without Mum noticing. It will be ruined!"

Chapter Eight
Party Time at the Rescue Zoo!

When Zoe woke up on Saturday morning, the first thing that popped into her head was her mum's birthday, and the party they were throwing. "It's today!" she said happily to Meep, a huge grin spreading over her face. "Mum's birthday party is today!"

 77

Usually Zoe had to persuade the little lemur to get out of bed with promises of a tasty breakfast – Meep loved snuggling up and snoozing under the cosy covers, especially in winter. But this morning he was already wide awake, perched on the windowsill. "I was too excited to sleep properly!" Meep explained, bouncing up and down. "Since your mum's already out in the zoo, can we go straight to the polar bear enclosure and start her birthday celebrations? There's lots to do, isn't there?"

Zoe giggled as she got out of bed, and scooped Meep up for a cuddle. "There's lots to do but we've got to do *our* jobs around the zoo first," she reminded him. "I promised to help feed the otters this morning. After that, we'll head over to the polar bear enclosure!"

"I can't wait to see all the decorations in place," Meep chattered eagerly.

"Me too, Meep," said Zoe. "Thank goodness Snowy ate a little bit of fish yesterday, so Mum doesn't have to go back and check on her today. She'd spot the balloons and the bunting, and the surprise would be ruined!"

After a quick breakfast of porridge for Zoe and a chopped-up banana for Meep, they wrapped up warm and set off into the zoo, ready to do their jobs for the morning. Zoe wanted to wish her mum happy birthday, but in a way she was glad they didn't bump into her. Zoe and Meep were so excited that if they had, her mum might have guessed that something was going on!

 79

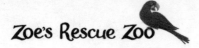

Zoe hummed a happy tune as she threw handfuls of shiny silver fish to the hungry otters. Meep bounced around like a jack-in-the-box, turning excited cartwheels, and even when Benedict the otter accidentally splashed him, the little lemur didn't mind.

Finally they set off down the path for Bella and Snowy's enclosure. All around them, the Rescue Zoo animals were excitedly chattering about Lucy's birthday too. Lots of them wished they could come to the party themselves, but Zoe had suggested they could all celebrate in their own enclosures anyway.

The hippos were having a mud party, and the birds of paradise had been practising a special birthday song, and explained to Zoe that they would sing

it as Lucy walked past. And the clever
chimps had made party hats out of the
palm leaves that grew in their enclosure,
and planned to wear them all day.

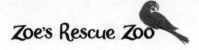

Zoe grinned as she saw all the animals'
celebrations. Even though her mum
wouldn't know that they were doing it
for her birthday, it really added to the
celebratory atmosphere around the zoo!

When Zoe arrived at the polar bear
enclosure, Great-Uncle Horace, the
zookeepers and lots of her
mum's friends were
already there. "Wow
– it looks amazing.
Like a real winter
wonderland!"
breathed Zoe,
looking around.
The enclosure
was dotted with
bunches of white
and blue balloons,

and the fir trees were strung with fairy
lights. Zoe's home-made bunting hung
across the entrance to the igloo.

Inside, a table on the viewing platform was covered in delicious-looking party food. There were gingerbread snowmen, brownies cut into the shape of snowflakes and dusted with icing sugar, and dishes of wobbly blue jelly and ice cream.

In the middle was a huge white chocolate cake in the shape of an igloo – just like the one they were in! To drink there was warm apple juice with cinnamon, or hot chocolate with whipped cream and marshmallows.

"Mmmm!" Zoe suddenly felt *very* hungry. "It almost looks too good to eat."

"*Almost*," squeaked Meep, looking eagerly at a dish of blueberries.

Zoe scooped him up for a cuddle. "It's not time to tuck in just yet, Meep," she whispered, laughing. "We have to wait for

84

Mum to arrive!"

The polar bears were both in the
swimming pool, below the viewing
platform. Zoe was glad to see that
they were splashing around together,
practising the show that Snowy had
talked about! She grinned as Snowy

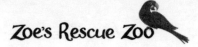

turned a somersault under the water and
Bella copied her. But when Bella came
to the surface to suggest a new move —
swimming down to the bottom of the
pool and touching the floor — Snowy
shook her head, barking and squealing
bossily. The little cub was sure that *her*
ideas were the best! Bella looked cross,
and when Great-Uncle Horace and the
guests were busy putting up a HAPPY
BIRTHDAY banner, Zoe sneaked away
and went down to the pool. She called
quietly over to Bella while Snowy was
practising a move under water.

"Is everything OK?" she asked quickly.

Bella barked back grumpily and Zoe
nodded, feeling very sorry for her friend.
"I know — Snowy isn't very good at
listening," she agreed. "I can see why

you're so annoyed. But you know that
Snowy is only behaving like this because
she wants to impress you, don't you?"

Bella looked surprised, and gave a
curious bark. Zoe smiled as she realised
something. "I think she just wants to be
your friend, Bella. Snowy's come to a new
place where she doesn't know anyone.
She probably looks up to a bigger, older
bear like you, and wants you to like her.
Maybe if you don't get so annoyed with
her, she'll calm down and stop being so
pesky. Will you try?"

Bella hesitated for a moment, and
looked across the pool at the little cub.
Snowy had bobbed up to the surface
and was waiting hopefully, looking at
the bigger bear with eager, dark eyes.
Then Bella nodded, and Zoe grinned

87

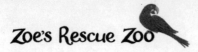
in relief. "Thanks, Bella. Now, I'd better go and fetch my mum – it's time for the party to start!"

Chapter Six
Mr Pinch Steps In!

"Oh no, Zoe! Mr Pinch is coming this way!" hissed Meep as they slipped out of the polar bear enclosure. "What if he's changed his mind about the party?"

Zoe's heart sank. Mr Pinch was marching towards them, a very determined expression on his face – which was exactly how he looked whenever he

89

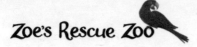

was about to stop them having fun. "He can't make us cancel it now. Everybody is here and the party's all set up," Zoe whispered back — but she couldn't help feeling worried.

"Zoe!" barked Mr Pinch. "Just the person I was looking for."

Zoe crossed her fingers tightly. "Mr Pinch! I promise we haven't made a mess—" she began, but Mr Pinch was shaking his head.

"I wasn't coming to tell you off. I was coming to tell you that your mum is heading this way to check on the polar bears!" he explained.

Zoe stared at him in surprise. Mr Pinch was trying to help! "But the guests won't have hidden yet. They're supposed to jump out and surprise her," she said.

"What shall we do?"

Mr Pinch looked thoughtful for a moment. "I know, I'll stop her!" he cried. "I'll say I need to talk to her about an important zoo matter. That should buy us a little bit of time – but you'd better tell everyone to get ready, quick!"

"Thank you, Mr Pinch," Zoe said gratefully, and the zoo manager blushed.

"Err – you're welcome," he said awkwardly.

"See you at the party!" she said with a smile.

"Oh . . . yes!" he said, sounding a little surprised that he was invited. He smiled back at her briefly and then rushed off.

Zoe dashed back inside the enclosure and popped her head into the igloo. Great-Uncle Horace and all the guests

91

were chatting excitedly, and someone had put some cheerful party music on.

"Quick, everyone – Mum's on her way!" Zoe called. "Mr Pinch is going to keep her busy for another minute or two, but you all need to hide, and stay really quiet. When she arrives, I'll say 'NOW!' and everyone can jump out and shout, 'HAPPY BIRTHDAY!'"

Great-Uncle Horace nodded enthusiastically. "Understood, Zoe! Come on, everyone – turn the music off, please, and get into your hiding places!"

Zoe giggled as Great-Uncle Horace and the other zookeepers squeezed under the table, squashed against the side of the big ice columns, and ducked behind the door.

When Zoe went back outside she could

hear voices along the path. Mr Pinch was doing his very best not to let Lucy inside the polar-bear enclosure!

"So, I have some important news that I need to tell you," he was saying.

"Well, what is it, Mr Pinch?" Lucy asked. "Perhaps we could talk about it later. I'm on my way to visit the polar bears."

"NO! I mean, err, no, wait a moment," blustered Mr Pinch. "It's very

93

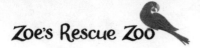

important. You see. . .err . . . Well, we have
a new kind of seed to feed to the parrots.
Yes, that's it! It just arrived today, much
cheaper than the old kind but just as
good. . . Anyway, I just thought you'd like
to know."

"That's very interesting, Mr Pinch," said
Lucy, giving him a strange look. "Thank
you for telling me."

"Good old Mr Pinch," whispered Zoe
to Meep. "He helped to save the surprise!"

She stepped out of the enclosure and
smiled at the zoo manager, who was
looking very flustered. "Hi, Mum," she
said. "I'm glad you're coming to visit the
polar bears. There's something you should
see inside the igloo!"

Mr Pinch looked very relieved that he
could stop pretending! Zoe smiled to

thank him, and he followed on behind them as Zoe led her mum into the enclosure.

"What is it, Zoe?" Lucy asked curiously. "Are the polar bears all right?"

"They're fine, Mum. You'll see," Zoe told her, grinning.

Looking very puzzled, Lucy stepped inside the igloo – and just as she did, Zoe cried, "NOW!"

Everyone burst out from their hiding places all at once, yelling, "HAPPY BIRTHDAY!"

Great-Uncle Horace let off a party popper, and Lucy gasped, looking around at all her friends gathered there. Zoe grinned as her mum saw all the balloons and decorations, and the yummy party food laid out on the table.

95

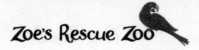
"Oh my goodness! What a surprise!" she laughed. "How lovely, everyone – I didn't expect a birthday party! Thank you!"

"You should thank Zoe, who organised every single detail," Great-Uncle Horace told her, beaming. "She knew you'd love a surprise, and she made all the decorations and organised this delicious food."

"It's the best present I could have asked for," Lucy said happily, hugging Zoe. "And the party food looks wonderful! Shall we tuck in?"

Soon everyone was enjoying the delicious cake, gingerbread men, hot chocolate and cinnamon apple juice, and Zoe put the music on again so that everyone could dance.

"And now it's time for the polar bears to put on their special show," Zoe whispered

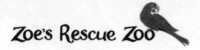

to Meep. "I just hope they don't fall out with each other again!"

Zoe slipped away from the party and crept down from the viewing platform to the edge of the swimming pool, where Bella and Snowy were waiting. "Are you ready?" she asked the polar bears quietly. "I can't wait to see this!"

Bella nodded, but Snowy bounced eagerly up and down, yapping excitedly. "Be careful, Snowy," Zoe warned. "You're right next to the snow—"

Before she could finish her sentence, Snowy lost her balance – and fell with a thump against the snow machine! Suddenly there was a noisy whirring, and the soft spray of snowflakes that poured out of the machine to cover the enclosure became a thick cloud. "Oh no," gasped

Zoe. "Snowy, you've created a blizzard!"

Snowy looked anxiously at all the extra snow that was starting to fall. Already it was piling up on the banks of the swimming pool, higher and higher, and Zoe knew that Great-Uncle Horace or her mum would notice it at any moment. But to Zoe's surprise, Bella gave Snowy a reassuring little nudge with her nose and barked happily.

"Maybe you're right, Bella," said Zoe thoughtfully. "It might make the party extra wintry! But I think I should try to fix the machine while you two are doing your show. Why don't you start and Meep can get everyone's attention!"

As Zoe bent over the snow machine, trying to understand which buttons would change how quickly the snow fell, the bears stood next to each other on the edge of the pool. Meep sprang nimbly up to the viewing platform and landed on Great-Uncle Horace's shoulder, tugging at his collar and pointing down at the pool with a tiny finger.

"Goodness, look down there!" Zoe heard Great-Uncle Horace call to the party guests. "It seems as though our wonderful polar bears are about to perform for us."

The crowd gasped and cheered as Bella and Snowy splashed eagerly into the water. They turned somersaults, dived underwater and splashed back to the surface. Zoe grinned as they did the diving move Bella had suggested, too! Then Snowy hopped on to Bella's back and barked happily, as Bella glided

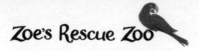

around the pool in circles.

Just as the bears got to their final move, Zoe spotted the right button to press on the snow machine. "That's it!" she whispered, breathing a sigh of relief as the snow once again fell gently and slowly.

As the bears swam back to the edge of the pool and splashed out, their audience giving them a huge round of applause, Zoe was waiting for them. "You were brilliant!" she whispered happily. "And the party guests enjoyed your show so much, they didn't even notice the extra snow storm!"

Chapter Ten
Making Friends

Everyone had loved the bears' show —
especially Lucy. Afterwards, Zoe heard
her mum cheering loudly and telling
Great-Uncle Horace, "That was brilliant!
This is the best birthday I've ever had."

"Perhaps it's time for you to cut the
birthday cake, my dear?" suggested Great-
Uncle Horace. "I'll light the candles!"

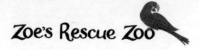

As the crowd gathered around the cake,
Zoe ran to the edge of swimming pool.
"You were amazing!" she whispered to
the polar bears. "You worked together,
like real friends always do. I'm so proud
of you both." She winked at Bella secretly,
proud that the older bear had been so
patient with Snowy.

The little cub gave a bashful squeak, and Zoe smiled. "It *is* important to listen, Snowy," she agreed, "and I know you will always try to let others have a turn from now on. But your ideas for the party made it even more fun, and it wouldn't have been the same without you. My mum loved the show!"

Snowy barked happily, and Bella nuzzled her little friend fondly. Zoe grinned at them both. "I'd better get back to the party before anyone notices I'm missing," she said. "I'll come and see you tomorrow."

Back up on the viewing platform, Lucy was blowing out her candles on the chocolate igloo cake, which was covered in delicious thick white icing to make it look like packed snow. She cut it, and

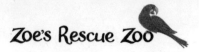

then Great-Uncle Horace handed out slices of cake to everyone. Even Mr Pinch nibbled one, and chatted happily to some of the zookeepers. "I don't usually like parties," he explained. "But this one has been rather nice, I must admit!"

The next day Zoe and Meep went back to the polar bear enclosure – and this time they had a surprise for Bella and Snowy! Zoe carried a bucket full of Bella's favourite fish, with a big red bow tied to the handle, and Meep pushed along a brand-new bouncy ball for Snowy.

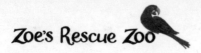

"They're thank-you presents," Zoe explained as the bears barked excitedly, and grinned as Bella shared her fish with Snowy. "For helping Mum's party go so well – *and* for making friends with each other!"

Meep giggled as Snowy bounced the ball to Bella, squeaking eagerly, and Bella chased after it. "It's nice to see them so happy now, Zoe," he chirped.

"I know," agreed Zoe, picking Meep up for a cuddle.

"I wonder what animal Goo will bring back to the Rescue Zoo next?" Meep wondered.

Zoe smiled. "I don't know. He's setting off on his next adventure tomorrow. I can't wait to see what he comes home with."

"It could be a warthog,
or a rhino, or a lizard,
or a leopard," Meep
said. "Or even
another polar
bear!"

"Yes! I'm sure
Snowy would love
making another new
friend now, she's got the
hang of it," Zoe said, grinning at the
fluffy polar bear. "Whatever the animal is,
I'm sure it's going to be a lot of fun!"

If you enjoyed Snowy's story,
look out for:

Zoe's Rescue ZOO

The Puzzled Penguin

Chapter One
Summer at the Rescue Zoo!

Zoe Parker grinned as she ran out of the school gates, swinging her bag beside her. Her mum, Lucy, was waiting for her. "It's the summer holidays!" Zoe yelled, giving her mum a big hug.

Lucy smiled and ruffled her daughter's wavy brown hair. "How was the last day of term?" she asked.

Zoe began to skip excitedly along the pavement. "It was fun, but I just couldn't wait for the holidays to start. Six whole weeks!" She smiled at her mum. "And I get to spend every single day at my favourite place."

As they got closer to home Zoe heard noises ahead: roars, bellows, screeches and squeaks. Animal noises!

Finally they turned a corner, and there in front of them stood a pair of tall, beautiful gates, with a line of lush oak trees on either side. The gates were made of golden wood, and covered with delicate carvings of every sort of animal you could think of. There were majestic tigers, soaring eagles, snapping crocodiles and elegant gazelles. About halfway up, two words were carved across the gates in swirling letters: RESCUE ZOO. Right at the top, a golden hot-air balloon twinkled in the sunlight.

A queue of excited visitors were streaming through the gates, but Zoe and her mum walked straight past them. As she stepped inside the zoo, a familiar warm, happy feeling spread through Zoe's tummy. "Home sweet home," she whispered.

Zoe and her mum weren't visiting the zoo – they *lived* there! Zoe's Great-Uncle Horace was a famous explorer and animal expert, and on his travels around the world he had met lots of animals in need of help. That was why he'd decided to build the zoo, so it could be a safe place for any creature who was lost, injured or in trouble. Now it was home to hundreds of amazing animals!

Zoe's mum was Horace's niece, and the zoo vet. She and Zoe lived in a little cottage on the edge of the zoo, so that Lucy could be there whenever the animals needed her. Zoe couldn't imagine a better place to live!

Beyond the gates, a red-brick path wound its way through the zoo. On a warm summer's day like this, there were hundreds of visitors, chattering as they wandered past each enclosure. Now that school had finished, lots of families were starting to arrive. Zoe spotted Jack and Nicola from her class, still in their green-and-white school uniforms. She smiled and waved at them, and they waved back.

"That's Zoe, the girl I told you about,"

she heard Jack telling his dad. "She lives here. It's so cool!"

As Zoe and her mum made their way through the crowds to their cottage, Zoe heard an excited chattering noise above her. She looked up, shading her eyes from the bright sunlight. From the top of a sycamore tree, a tiny, furry face peeped cheekily down at her.

"Meep!" called Zoe, smiling. "Come down from there, you cheeky thing!"

With a swift leap, the little creature bounded down and landed nimbly on Zoe's shoulder. Zoe gathered the soft, warm bundle into her arms for a cuddle. Meep was a tiny grey mouse lemur with enormous golden eyes and a long, velvety tail. Great-Uncle Horace had rescued him when he was just a baby, and had

brought him to the Rescue Zoo. Now
Meep lived in the cottage with Zoe, and
was her very best friend.

"Meep has been especially mischievous
today," Lucy told Zoe as they continued
along the path. "Mr Pinch brought a
very tasty-looking blueberry muffin
in this morning for his breakfast. Then
this week's fruit delivery arrived and
he went to supervise it. When he came
back, his muffin was gone. Mr Pinch was
very cross." She shook her head at the
little lemur. "He didn't know what had
happened to it, but *I* noticed that Meep's
paws were covered in crumbs!"

Zoe couldn't help laughing, and hugged
Meep closer. Mr Pinch was the zoo
manager, and was *always* grumpy. Meep
loved teasing him!

As they arrived at the cottage, Lucy handed Zoe's school bag back to her. "I've got to go and check on a leopard now, so I'll leave you two to have fun. Be home in time for tea." She planted a quick kiss on Zoe's head and tickled Meep's soft little belly.

"OK, Mum!" Zoe smiled as she watched Lucy dash away towards the zoo hospital.

Once she was out of sight, Zoe stepped inside the cottage and grinned at Meep. The cheeky little lemur leaped from her shoulder and scampered over to the bowl of fruit on the kitchen table. "Yummy!" he chirped, peeling a banana with his nimble fingers. "Blueberry muffins are nice, but I like bananas best."

Zoe giggled. It was always fun to be by herself with Meep, or any of the animals at the Rescue Zoo. When other people weren't around, she didn't have to hide their amazing secret.

Zoe knew that animals could talk to people, and that just a few special people could talk back to them. And she was one of them!

Look out for more amazing animal adventures at the Rescue Zoo!

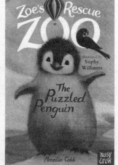

The Rescue Princesses

Have you read them all?

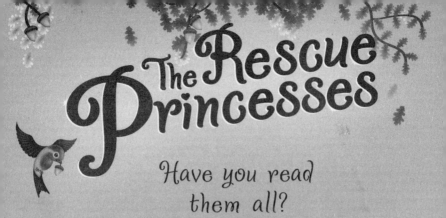

nosy crow